THE SECRET GARDEN

To the ability to change and blossom

&

to my wife, Suzanne Ramljak

R. S.

© 2001 by Running Press
Illustrations © 2001 by Robert Sauber

All rights reserved under the Pan-American
and International Copyright Conventions

Printed in China

9   8   7   6   5   4   3
Digit on the right indicates the number of this printing

Library of Congress Cataloging-in-Publication Number 00-135107

ISBN 0-7624-0572-4

Designed and illustrated by Robert Sauber
Edited by Melissa Wagner
Typography: Goudy, Goodfellow, and Terminus

This book may be ordered by mail from the publisher.
But try your bookstore first!

Published by Courage Books, an imprint of
Running Press Book Publishers
125 South Twenty-second Street
Philadelphia, Pennsylvania 19103-4399

Visit us on the web!
www.runningpress.com

THE SECRET GARDEN

By

Frances
Hodgson Burnett

Illustrated by

Robert Sauber

Retold by

Jane Parker Resnick

COURAGE
BOOKS
AN IMPRINT OF RUNNING PRESS
PHILADELPHIA • LONDON

CONTENTS

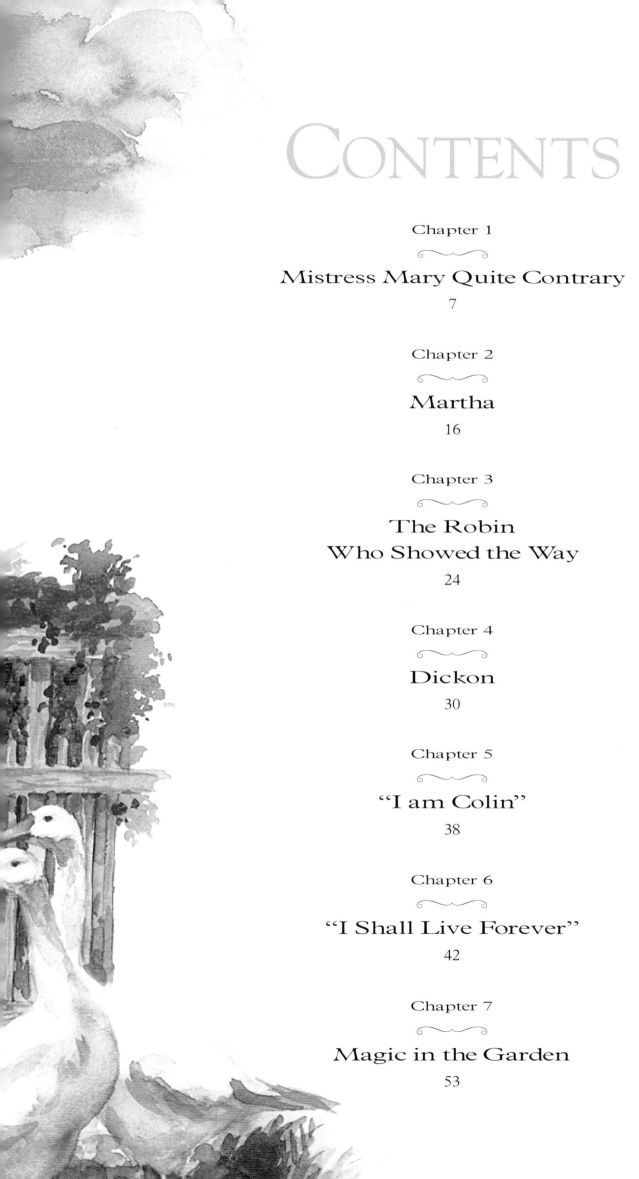

Chapter 1

Mistress Mary Quite Contrary

When Mary Lennox was sent to Misselthwaite Manor to live with her uncle, everybody said she was the most disagreeable-looking child ever seen. It was true, too. She had a little thin face, a thin body, thin light hair, and a sour expression. Her face was yellow because she had always been ill.

She had been born in India while her father was working there for the English government. Her mother had been a great beauty who cared only for parties. She had not wanted a little girl at all.

When Mary was born, her mother handed her over to an Ayah, an Indian servant, and told her to keep the child out of sight. The servants gave Mary her own way and she became as bossy and selfish a little pig as ever lived.

One awful morning when Mary was nine years old, she awoke to the sound of wailing among the servants and hurrying footsteps. A terrible disease called cholera had broken out and people were dying everywhere. Her Ayah was the first in the household to die.

Mary was frightened and stayed in her room crying and sleeping all through that day and night.

When Mary awakened the next day, the house was still. She wondered who would take care of her now that her Ayah was dead. She did not cry because her nurse had died. Mary had never cared much for anyone. She was angry because no one seemed to remember she was alive.

Then she heard footsteps coming toward the nursery, and an officer opened the door.

Mary was standing in the middle of the room. She looked like an ugly, cross little thing. She was frowning because she was hungry and feeling neglected. The man was so startled when he saw her that he almost jumped back.

"Who are you?" he asked.

"I am Mary Lennox. Why does nobody come?" she said, stamping her foot.

"Poor little kid!" the man said. "There is nobody left to come."

It was in that strange, sudden way that Mary found out that she had neither father nor mother. She was the only one left alive in the house.

At first Mary stayed with an English family with five children. She hated it there and was so disagreeable that no one played with her. The boy, Basil, watched her digging in the garden alone and gave her a nickname, "Mistress Mary Quite Contrary."

He laughed and sang:

"Mistress Mary, quite contrary,

How does your garden grow?

With silver bells, and cockle shells,

And marigolds all in a row."

Then Mary was sent to England to live with her uncle, Archibald Craven. She was met in London by Mrs. Medlock, the housekeeper of Misselthwaite Manor. Mary didn't like Mrs. Medlock, but she seldom liked anyone, and Mrs. Medlock didn't care for her either.

"My word! She's a plain piece of goods!" Mrs. Medlock thought as they boarded the train for Yorkshire.

"You are going to a queer place," said Mrs. Medlock.

Mary pretended not to be interested.

"It's grand in a gloomy way. The house is six hundred years old and it's on the edge of
the moor. There's near a hundred rooms in it, though most of them's locked up. There's a big
park and gardens all around."

It sounded so unlike India that Mary was interested in spite of herself. But she said nothing.

"Well, don't you care?" Mrs. Medlock asked.

"It doesn't matter," said Mary, "if I care or not."

"You're right," Mrs. Medlock replied. "He's not going to trouble himself about you.
He's got a crooked back," she said. "He was a sour young man until he married and then when
his wife died, it made him queerer than ever. He cares about nobody. He won't see people.
Most of the time he's away."

It began to rain. Mary turned her face toward the window and gazed out at the gray storm. She had once read a fairy tale about a poor hunchback and a beautiful princess, and suddenly she felt sorry for her uncle.

"And you'll have to play about and look after yourself," Mrs. Medlock went on. "There won't be people to talk to you. And you'll have to stay in certain rooms. You can't go poking about."

"I won't," said Mary. And just as suddenly as she had begun to be sorry for Mr. Craven, she stopped and began to think that he was unpleasant enough to deserve all that had happened to him.

Mary and Mrs. Medlock got off the train at Thwaite Station and were taken from there by carriage. Mary looked out the window.

"What's a moor?" she asked.

"It's just miles of wild land that nothing grows on but heather and broom," Mrs. Medlock said. "Nothing lives on it but wild ponies and sheep."

The wind was making a low, rushing sound. The moor seemed to Mary like a bleak, dark sea.

They arrived at an enormous house that seemed almost completely dark. A man met them at the door.

"You are to take her to her room," he said. "He doesn't want to see her. He's going to London tomorrow."

Then Mary was led up staircases and down corridors until a door opened onto a room with a fire and a supper on a table.

"This room and the next are where you'll live—and you must keep to them," Mrs. Medlock said. "Don't forget that!"

Chapter 2

Martha

ary was awakened by Martha, the young maid. She looked out the window
to see a great climbing stretch of land.

"What is that?" she asked.

"That's th' moor," Martha answered. "It's bare now, but fair lovely in the spring an' summer when the flowers is growin' and the skylarks makes such a noise singin."

"Who will dress me?" Mary said haughtily.

"Canna' the' dress thysen!" Martha said in her broad Yorkshire accent.

"No," answered Mary, indignantly. "My Ayah dressed me of course."

"Well," said Martha, "it's time the' should learn."

By the time Mary was dressed she suspected her life at Misselthwaite Manor would teach her a great many new things. Martha told her to go outside and play.

"If the' goes round the' way tha'll come to th' gardens," she said. "One of them's locked up. No one has been in it for ten years."

"Why?" asked Mary.

"Mr. Craven had it shut when his wife died so sudden. It was her garden. He locked th' door an' dug a hole and buried th' key."

Mary could not help thinking about the garden where no one had been for ten years. She wondered what it would look like and whether there were any flowers alive in it. She walked through the main gardens to the ivy-covered walls of the kitchen gardens. The place had the bare look of winter.

She kept on through an orchard. The wall seemed to go beyond the orchard, but there was no door. She could see the treetops on the other side and a bird with a bright red breast sitting on a branch.

Suddenly he burst into his winter song—almost as if he was calling to her.

Even though she was "Mistress Mary Quite Contrary," the bright-breasted bird brought a look into her sour little face which was almost a smile. She listened until he flew away.

"I feel sure that tree was in the secret garden," she said. "There was a wall 'round the place and there was no door."

Back in the kitchen gardens, Mary came upon
an old gardener, Ben Weatherstaff. At first he ignored her.

"I saw a bird with a red breast on a tree in the garden
that has no door," she told him.

A slow smile spread over the gardener's face.
He began to whistle a low, soft whistle. Almost the
next moment, the bird with the red breast flew
to them and landed quite near the gardener.

"Where has the' been, the' cheeky little beggar?"
he said to the bird, as if he was speaking to a child.

The bird put his head on one side and looked up at him with his soft
dark eye. It gave Mary a queer feeling in her heart, because he was so pretty
and so like a person.

"What kind of bird is he?" Mary asked.

"He's a robin redbreast an' they're th' friendliest, curiousest birds alive.
He's th' only friend I've got."

"I have no friends at all," said Mary.

Suddenly the robin landed on a tree branch near Mary and burst into song.
Ben laughed.

"He's made up his mind to make friends with thee," he said.

"Would you make friends with me?" she said to the robin, just as if she was speaking
to a person. "Would you?" And she did not say it in her hard little voice, but in a soft,
sweet way.

"The' said that as nice as if the' was a real child instead of a sharp old woman," Ben said.
"The' said it almost like Dickon talks to his wild things on th' moor."

"Who's Dickon?" Mary asked.

"He's Martha's twelve-year-old brother," he replied. "Everybody knows him. All th'
animals an' birds on the moor are his friends."

Mary was as curious about Dickon as she was about the garden. But just then the robin spread his wings and flew away.

"He has flown over the wall to the garden with no door!" she cried.

"He lives there among the rose-trees," Ben said.

"I should like to see them," said Mary. "There must be a door!"

"None as anyone can find, an' none as is anyone's business," Ben said sternly. "Don't poke your nose where it's no cause to go."

And he threw his spade over his shoulder and walked off.

Every day Mary went out. She became stronger and began to eat better.

She often went to the wall where she saw the robin. Once she heard a brilliant chirp, and there he was.

"Is it you?" she cried out. She was so glad, she looked almost pretty.

"I like you!" she called, and tried to whistle.

The robin flew over the wall to the top of a tree.

"You're in the garden no one can go into, aren't you?" Mary said. "I wish I could see it!"

That night she asked Martha about the garden. The maid explained that Mr. Craven's wife died there. She was sitting on a branch that bent like a bench, with roses all around. She fell and hurt herself so badly that she died the next day.

"No one's allowed in since, " Martha said.

A storm was beginning and the wind howled. Suddenly Mary heard a sound like a child crying.

"Do you hear anyone crying?" she asked.

Martha looked confused. "No," she answered. "It's the wind."

But something in her manner made Mary stare at her. She did not believe Martha was speaking the truth.

Chapter 3

The Robin who Showed the Way

The next day it poured. There could be no going out.

"What do they do in your family's cottage when it rains?" Mary asked Martha.

"Try to keep from under each other's feet," she replied. "Except Dickon. He's out on the moor. Once he brought home a fox cub nearly drowned and another time a young crow. He's still got them."

Mary was very curious about Dickon. She couldn't explore the moor, she thought, but she could explore the house. She wandered all day down long corridors, through gloomy rooms. Suddenly she heard a cry.

"It's nearer than last night," thought Mary. "It is crying!" Then she saw Mrs. Medlock coming toward her with a cross look on her face.

"What are you doing here?" she said.

"I heard someone crying," Mary answered.

"You didn't hear anything," said the housekeeper. She dragged Mary back to her room. "Stay where you're told," she said, "or you'll be locked up."

Mary was pale with rage. "There was someone crying—there was!" she thought. "And I'll find out who!"

The next morning, Mary awoke to a deep blue sky above the moor. She rushed out to the garden to feel the crisp air. Ben Weatherstaff greeted her.

"Springtime's comin'," he said. "Cannot the' smell the rich earth? The flowers will be stirrin' below in th' dark. You'll see green spikes stickin' out soon. Crocuses an' daffydowndillys."

Suddenly Mary heard rustling wings. The robin had come.

"Are things stirring in the garden where he lives?" Mary asked. She wanted so much to know.

"Ask him," said Ben. "No one else's been inside for ten years."

Mary went to walk outside the ivy-covered wall over which she could see the treetops.
Then the most exciting thing happened.

She heard a chirp and a twitter and there was the robin hopping about. He had followed
her! Mary was so surprised and delighted that she almost trembled.

"You do remember me!" she cried. She chirped and coaxed and he hopped and flicked
his tail. It was as if he were talking. Mistress Mary forgot that she had ever been contrary
when he allowed her to draw closer and closer to him. She scarcely dared to breathe. The
robin hopped over a pile of freshly turned earth by the wall where a dog had dug a hole. He
stopped on it to look for a worm. Mary saw something almost buried there. It looked like a
ring of rusty iron. But it was more; it was an old key! She gasped and picked it up.

"Perhaps it has been buried for ten years," she whispered. "Perhaps it is the key to
the garden!"

Mary looked at the key quite a long time. She thought that if the key was to the
closed garden, and she could find out where the door was, she could open it and see what
was inside the walls.

Because the garden had been shut up for so long, Mary yearned to see it. She imagined that it must be different from other places, and perhaps it could be her own secret place. That thought pleased her. Mary put the key in her pocket and went to the house. She vowed to keep the key with her always, so that if she ever found the hidden door, she would be ready.

Martha had brought her a present—a skipping rope. Mary took it to the ivy-covered wall and began to skip along the path. And there was the robin again! He flew to a spray of ivy and sang a loud, lovely trill.

Mary had heard about Magic in her Ayah's stories, and she had always said that what

happened next *was* Magic.

    She stepped close to the robin. A gust of wind lifted the ivy and she saw something under it—a doorknob! Mary's heart began to thump with excitement. She pulled the leaves aside . . . and found the lock.

    She took the key from her pocket—it fit in the lock! She turned the key and opened the door ever so slowly. Then she slipped through the door, shut it, and stood with her back against it, looking around with wonder and delight.

    She was standing *inside* the secret garden.

Chapter 4

Dickon

It was the sweetest, most mysterious place anyone could imagine. It was the climbing roses that made the garden look so strange and lovely. Their tendrils had spread onto the trees and hung down in hazy curtains everywhere.

"Is it all quite dead?" Mary wondered. "I hope it isn't." Then she noticed some little green points sticking out of the earth.

"These might be crocuses or daffodils," she whispered.

But the grass was so thick that the green points hardly seemed to have room to grow. She found a stick and dug clear places around them. She worked happily all day.

At dinner she told Martha she wished she could buy a spade to dig her own garden.

"Dickon can make flowers grow out of a brick walk," Martha said. "He'll bring you a spade and some flower seeds."

"Oh!" exclaimed Mary, "I want to see him very much!"

That night Mary heard that far-off cry again.

"That's three times," she thought. But she was so tired from the day's excitement that she could not keep awake.

The sun shone for a week on Mary's secret garden. Shut up in its old walls, Mary felt like she was in a fairy place. She was determined to make the garden come alive and worked hard clearing spaces around the flowers' green shoots. If no one found out about the garden, Mary thought, she would enjoy it herself always.

One day she heard a whistling sound in a park near the garden. There she found a boy with the reddest cheeks and the roundest blue eyes playing on a wooden pipe. Two rabbits crept close to him. Mary knew at once that he was Dickon.

"I know tha'rt Miss Mary," he said. "I've brought the tools and seeds."

Dickon told her the seeds were mignonette. "The sweetest smellin' thing as grows." Then he turned his head quickly and his face lit up.

"Where's that robin callin' us?" he asked. "He's callin' someone he's friends with."

"He's Ben's," Mary said.

"He knows thee, too," Dickon said. "He likes thee."

Dickon moved close to the bush where the robin was and made a sound almost like the bird's own. The robin answered.

"Aye, he's a friend o' yours," Dickon chuckled.

Mary could hardly believe it, but Dickon said he talked to all the animals this way.

"Where is the' garden?" he asked. "I'll plant the seeds for thee."

Mary went red and then pale.

"Could you keep a secret?" she said. "I believe I would die if anyone found out."

"I'm keepin' the animals' secrets always," Dickon replied.

"I've stolen a garden," she said quickly. "I don't care," she shouted. "Nobody has a right to take it from me when I care about it and they don't!" Then she burst out crying.

Dickon's curious blue eyes grew rounder. "Where is it?" he asked.

"I'll show you," she said. And she took him through the hidden door.

Dickon looked all around.

"Eh!" he whispered. "It's like a dream." Dickon walked throughout the garden.

"Will there be roses?" Mary whispered. "Are they dead?"

"Not all of 'em," Dickon answered. "Look here!" He cut into a brown branch with his knife, showing Mary the healthy green color inside.

"It's as live as you and me," he said.

"Let's count the live ones!" cried Mary.

Dickon was as eager as she. They spent the morning clearing around the live bushes giving them room to breathe. Dickon noticed the flower beds where Mary had worked.

"Tha' has done a lot o'work," he said.

"When I dig I'm not tired," said Mary. "I like to smell the earth when it's turned up. Will you come again and help?" she begged.

"Every day," he replied. "It's the best fun I ever had—shut in here an' wakenin' up a garden."

Mary liked Dickon. "That's four people I like," she thought. "Martha, Ben, Dickon, and the robin." That was a lot for a little girl who had never liked anyone.

She didn't feel contrary at all.

Mary ran back to the house to find Martha waiting for her.

"Mr. Craven's here," she said. "He wants to see you."

Mary was frightened. Perhaps, if he found out, he would take the garden away. When Mary entered his room, the pink left her cheeks. She felt like a thin, pale little girl again.

"Come here," he said. He was not ugly. He would have been handsome if it weren't for the sadness in his face. He was not a hunchback either, but had crooked shoulders.

"Are you well?" he asked.

"Yes," answered Mary.

"Do they take care of you?"

"Yes."

"Perhaps you need a governess."

"No!" Mary blurted. "Please . . . please."

"What?"

"May I have a bit of earth?" she asked.

"Earth!" he repeated. "What do you mean?"

"To make things grow . . . to see them come alive," Mary faltered.

"You can have as much earth as you want," he said. "You remind me of someone else who loved to see things grow." He almost smiled.

"May I take it anywhere—if it's not wanted?"

"Anywhere," he said. "I'll be leaving for a long time tomorrow. Go now."

Mary raced to her secret garden.

Chapter 5

"I Am Colin"

That night Mary woke to the crying sound she had heard before. Determined to find out what it was, she crept through the corridors to the door where the sound was clearest. She pushed open the door. On a bed was a boy who looked as if he might be ill.

"Who are you?" he asked. He stared at her with enormous gray eyes. "Are you a ghost?"

"I am Mary Lennox," she said. "Mr. Craven is my uncle."

"I am Colin," he said. "Mr. Craven is my father."

Mary gasped. "Why didn't anyone tell me he had a boy!"

"Because I'm always sick. I don't let anyone talk about me," he answered. "If I live I may be a hunchback, but I shan't live. No one believes I will grow up."

"Do you want to live?" Mary asked.

"No," he whined. "But I don't want to die. It makes me so cross to think about it, I cry and cry."

"Does your father come to see you?"

"Not often," Colin said. "It makes him sad to see me. My mother died just after I was born. He almost hates me. How old are you?"

"I'm ten," Mary said, "and so are you, because you were born when the garden was locked."

Colin sat up. "What garden?" he asked almost eagerly. He had had nothing to think about for so long. A hidden garden appealed to him.

"It's the garden Mr. Craven hates. No one's been allowed to go in for ten years," Mary said nervously.

"Where?" he demanded. "I can make the gardeners take me there."

"Oh, don't do that!" she cried. She was so afraid her secret would be spoiled. "If you make them take you in, it will never be a secret," she said. "If I can find it—and no one goes there but ourselves—we could play every day and plant seeds and make things come alive. It's nearly spring."

"What is spring like?" he asked. "I never go outside."

"It is the sun and rain and things pushing up under the earth. If the garden was a secret we could watch things."

"I should like that," he said.

And Mary told him how she thought the garden looked, and how the roses might be growing, and how the robin became her friend. And she promised to look for the key.

Poor Colin fell asleep dreaming of the secret garden.

The next day it was still raining. Mary told Martha she had found out about Colin. The poor maid was terrified that Mrs. Medlock would fire her.

"You won't lose your place," said Mary. "He was glad I came."

"You've bewitched him," Martha gasped. "Everyone's afraid of him—him and his tantrums."

"I'm not," Mary said. "He liked me. What's the matter with him?"

"When he was born, his father feared Colin would be another hunchback," Martha explained. "He isn't yet. But he's always kept lyin' down. Once a doctor from London said there'd been too much medicine an' too much lettin' him have his own say."

"I think he's very spoiled," Mary said.

Colin called Mary and Martha to his room. He spoke to Martha in such a grand manner that Mary just stared.

"I'll send Medlock away if she dares to fire you," he said. "I'll take care of you. Now go away."

"You remind me of the Rajah I saw in India," Mary said. "Everyone had to do what he said or I think they would have been killed."

Colin took out a book about India and they came to a picture of a snake charmer.

"I know a boy who can charm foxes and squirrels," Mary said. And she told him all about Dickon and his animals on the moor.

"I could never go on the moor," Colin said fretfully. "I am going to die."

"How do you know?" Mary asked. Colin seemed almost to be boasting and she was not sympathetic.

"The servants and doctors always whisper it," he said. "Except the doctor from London who said I might live if I put my mind to it."

Dickon would turn his mind to living, Mary thought. "Let's not talk about dying," Mary said. Then she told him about the way Dickon spoke to the robin and about the sun and the moor.

"How I wish I could see Dickon," Colin sighed.

They laughed and were happy together. Mary forgot that she was an unloved girl and Colin forgot that he was a sickly boy who believed he was going to die.

Chapter 6

"I Shall Live Forever!"

It rained for a week. Mary spent hours with Colin. She wondered if she could trust him with her secret.

The first morning Mary awoke to a blue sky, she raced to the secret garden. Dickon was already there.

The garden was coming alive with springtime—leaf buds grew on the rose branches, and thousands of new green points pushed through the earth. Mary and Dickon dug and pulled and laughed with joy.

"I'm so happy I can scarcely breathe!" Mary said.

Then she told him about Colin. "He's so afraid he'll become a hunchback," she explained. "He thinks that if he should feel a lump coming he would go crazy."

"If he was out here he wouldn't be watchin' for lumps on his back; he'd be watchin' for buds to break on the rosebushes, en' he'd likely be healthier," said Dickon. "I was wonderin' if us could get him to come out here."

"I've been wondering that myself," Mary replied. "I've wondered if he could keep a secret."

"It'd be good for him," Dickon said. "Us'd be just two children watch'n a garden grow, an' he'd be another. Two lads an' a little lass just lookin' on at the spring time. I warrant it'd be better than doctor's stuff."

Mary saw a flare of the red-breasted robin dart through the trees with something in his beak. "Why, he's nest buildin'," Dickon said. Dickon made a whistling call and the robin chirped to him.

"The' knows us won't trouble thee," he said to the robin. "Us is near bein' wild things ourselves. Us is nest buildin' too."

That day Mary was so eager to work in the garden that she didn't visit Colin. When she returned, Martha looked worried.

"I wish tha' gone to see Colin," she said. "He was nigh goin' into one of his tantrums."

Mary's lips pinched together. She was not used to considering other people's feelings. Why should she give up what she liked best, she wondered. She was feeling quite contrary when she marched into Colin's room.

"I waited all day," he cried. "You are a selfish thing!"

"You're the most selfish boy ever!" she answered.

"I'm not as selfish as you, because I'm ill," he snapped. "I'm sure there's a lump on my back and I'm going to die!"

"I don't believe it!" Mary shouted. "You just say that to make people sorry."

"Get out of my room!" he cried.

"I'm going and I won't come back!" she screamed. Mary was very angry. But later she remembered what Colin had told her—that most of his tantrums were because of his secret fear that a lump was growing on his spine.

"I said I would never come back," she thought, "but—perhaps I'll go in the morning."

That night Mary awakened to dreadful screams. She knew it was Colin having a tantrum, and she pulled the pillow over her head.

"He's so spoiled," she thought. "Someone ought to shake him."

Suddenly Colin's nurse burst into her room. "Colin's in hysterics," she said. "No one can stop him. Do try! He likes you."

Mary flew down the corridor and was feeling quite wicked when she got there.

"Stop!" she shouted. "You'll scream yourself to death!"

Colin's face was swollen and he was choking.

"I can't," he sobbed.

"You can!" Mary screamed. "It's just hysterics!"

"I felt the lump," he choked. "I shall have a hunch on my back and die."

"You didn't feel a lump!" Mary said fiercely. "Show me your back!"

Colin turned over and she looked at his thin back.

"There's not a lump as big as a pin," she insisted. Colin had never asked anyone about his secret fear before. Most of his illness was caused by fright. His back and legs were weak only because he never used them. No one had ever told him the truth before, but he was ready to believe this angry girl.

"Do you think I could live to grow up?" he asked the nurse.

"If you do what you're told and get a great deal of fresh air," she answered.

"I'll go out with you, Mary," he said, "if only we can find. . . ." He remembered just in time not to say "the secret garden."

Colin quieted down and the nurse left.

"Have you found the way into the garden?" he asked.

Mary looked at his tired face.

"Yes, I think I have," she said.

"Oh, Mary!" Colin said. "If I can get into it I think I shall live to grow up!"

Mary told him again how she imagined the garden looked, and he fell asleep at last.

The next morning Mary went to see Colin.

"I'm going to Dickon," she said. "I'll be back. I have something to tell you . . . about the garden."

Colin's tired face brightened.

Dickon was in the garden with his pet squirrels, Nut and Shell, his fox cub, Captain, and his crow, named Soot. Mary told him about Colin.

"We must get him out here," he said. "We must get him soaked up with sunshine. And we must lose no time."

Mary hated to leave, but she rushed back to Colin.

"You smell like flowers and fresh things!" he said.

She told him about Dickon and his animals.

"If only I could see them." Colin said.

"You can," Mary replied, "Dickon will come here tomorrow and bring all his creatures."

"Oh!" Colin cried in delight.

"And that's not all," Mary said. "Can I trust you? Can I trust you for sure?"

"Yes!" Colin said eagerly.

"I've found the door to the garden."

"Oh, Mary! I *shall* see it! Tell me about it!" And as Colin listened, all his aches and tiredness were forgotten.

The next morning Mary rushed to Colin's room.

"It's come!" she cried. "Spring! Dickon says so!"

"Open the window," Colin said.

Mary did, and freshness and scents and birds' songs poured in. "Breathe in the fresh air," she said. "Dickon says it makes him feel like he could live forever and ever!"

Colin took deep breaths. He felt as if something wonderful was happening to him.

"There are flowers and rosebushes everywhere in the garden," he said, "and birds rushing to finish their nests."

Then Dickon appeared carrying a newborn lamb. His fox trotted by his side. Nut and Soot sat on his shoulders, and Shell peeped out of his pocket.

Colin stared. He was so surprised he couldn't speak.

Dickon put the lamb in Colin's lap. "I brought it a bit hungry," he said and gave Colin a bottle to feed the lamb. Then Colin's questions came tumbling out and they talked and talked. They looked at a gardening book and Dickon pointed out the flowers that were coming up in the garden.

"I'm going to see them," Colin cried. "I am!"

They had to wait for a week because of windy weather. But they spent the time making secret plans for Colin's visit to the garden. He insisted that no one must know.

Finally, the day came. Colin was so excited. "This afternoon I shall be in it!" he sighed.

A servant carried Colin outside into his wheelchair and covered him with robes. Dickon pushed Colin and Mistress Mary walked beside him. Colin gazed up at the sky with his huge eyes.

As they approached the garden, they whispered.

"Here's where the robin showed me the key," Mary said. "It was Magic."

"Where!" Colin cried.

"This is where he chirped at me on the wall," Mary said. "And here's the ivy that blew back from the door."

"Oh!" gasped Colin.

Dickon guided the chair through the door with one firm push.

Colin looked round and round—at the trees and the rose bushes, the flowers and the birds. The sun warmed his face and a glow filled his pale cheeks.

"Mary! Dickon!" he cried. "I shall get well! I shall live forever and ever!"

Chapter 7

Magic in the Garden

That afternoon, Colin first felt the springtime inside a hidden garden. The world seemed perfect.

Mary and Dickon worked and brought him buds and twigs and a bird's feather.

"I don't want this afternoon to end," Colin said as the sun went down. "I'll come back every day. I'll watch everything grow. I'm going to grow here."

"Us'll have thee walkin' same as other folk soon," Dickon said.

"Walk?" Colin cried.

"The's got legs o' thine own," Dickon said.

"But they are so weak," Colin replied. "I'm afraid to stand."

"When the' stops bein' afraid tha'lt stand," Dickon said.

"Perhaps I can! Come here!" he shouted at Dickon.

Dickon ran to his side. Mary gasped.

"He can do it. The Magic can do it," she said to herself over and over again.

Dickon held Colin's arm. Colin put his thin legs out and stood upright—straight as an arrow!

"Look at me!" he cried.

And the Magic—or whatever it was— gave him such strength that when the sun set, Colin was standing on his own two feet—laughing!

In the weeks that followed, they always called it Magic. What amazing things happened in that garden! Buds bloomed into flowers. Roses spread everywhere.

Colin saw it all. He learned about birds and animals. And he thought about Magic.

One day he said, "I am going to try an experiment. Something is making things grow in this garden. I don't know its name so I call it Magic. I am going to try to get some Magic in me to make me strong."

Mary and Dickon listened closely.

They sat in a circle and Colin began to chant, "The sun is shining—that is Magic. The flowers are growing—that is Magic. Being alive is the Magic. The Magic is in me! Magic! Come and help!" He repeated the words over and over.

Then Colin announced, "I am going to walk around the garden."

Colin walked with Mary and Dickon at his sides. All Dickon's creatures followed them. Colin stopped to rest often, but he held his head high and he looked grand. He walked around the whole garden.

"I did it! I can feel it!" he cried. "The Magic worked!"

They kept their faith in the Magic. Colin made himself believe he would get well, and he did. In two months, he was digging and weeding in the garden. One day, Colin stood up from his work and stood very still. "Mary! Dickon!" he cried. "I just remembered the first day we came here. Now I can do everything. I'm well!" His face was filled with joy. "This is the biggest secret," he said. "No one must tell my father. When he returns I will walk into his study and say 'Here I am. I shall live to be a man.'"

"He won't believe his eyes," Mary said.

At the manor, Colin never walked. He pretended to have pains and Mary acted her part, too. "Poor Colin," she said, "does it hurt so much?"

In the garden, they laughed about their acting until they couldn't breathe. But they ate more and looked healthier and people noticed.

"The boy is a new creature," said Colin's nurse. "His skin is rosy. His eyes are bright!"

"So is the girl," added Mrs. Medlock. "She's downright pretty. She's filled out and lost her ugly, sour look. She and Colin laugh together like crazy young ones."

"It must be good," said the nurse. "Let them laugh!"

For ten years, Archibald Craven had grieved. He had lost his beautiful wife. He couldn't bear to look at his invalid son.

But one day, he was in a valley far from home that was so lovely his spirit could not resist its sweetness. He seemed to awaken. That night his wife's voice called to him in a dream.

"Archie! Archie!"

"Where are you?" he called back.

"In the garden," was the reply. The voice was so real that Archibald Craven returned home at once.

At Misselthwaite, he rushed to the hidden garden. "I don't know why, but I must find the key," he thought.

But when he reached the garden wall, he heard sounds of running feet and children laughing. Suddenly the door flew open and a boy burst through—almost into his arms.

"Who? Who are you!" he stammered in amazement.

"Father!" Colin cried in disbelief. "I'm Colin!"

"In the garden!" Mr Craven gasped.

"Yes," Colin hurried on. "It was the garden that did it—and Mary and Dickon and the creatures—and the Magic. I'm well! Aren't you glad, Father? I shall live forever and ever!"

Mr. Craven hugged Colin and held him.

"Take me into the garden," he said. "And tell me all about it."

And so they led him into the secret garden.

THE END